Q Pootle 5
IN SPACE!

NICK BUTTERWORTH

Collins

An imprint of HarperCollins*Publishers*

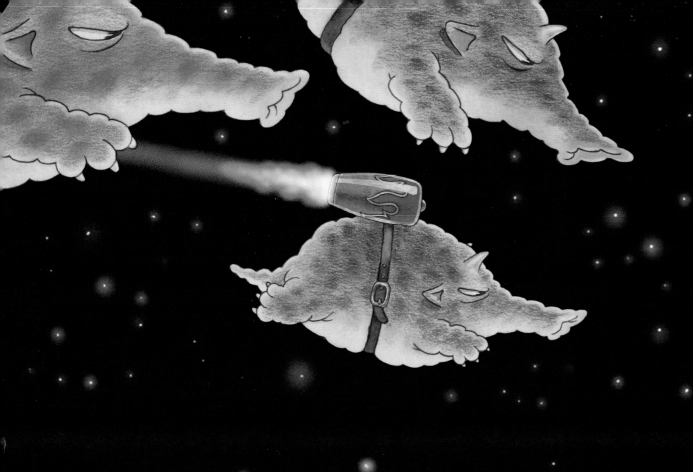

Q Pootle 5 is in a hurry. And so is his friend Oopsy. They were playing hide and seek but they have been found by three hungry bladder monsters.

The bladder monsters are having fun. But Q Pootle 5 and Oopsy don't like games like this. Not ones where you can get eaten.

The bladder monsters are huge. Much
bigger than Q Pootle 5 and Oopsy.
But Q Pootle 5 has a friend who is even
bigger than the bladder monsters.

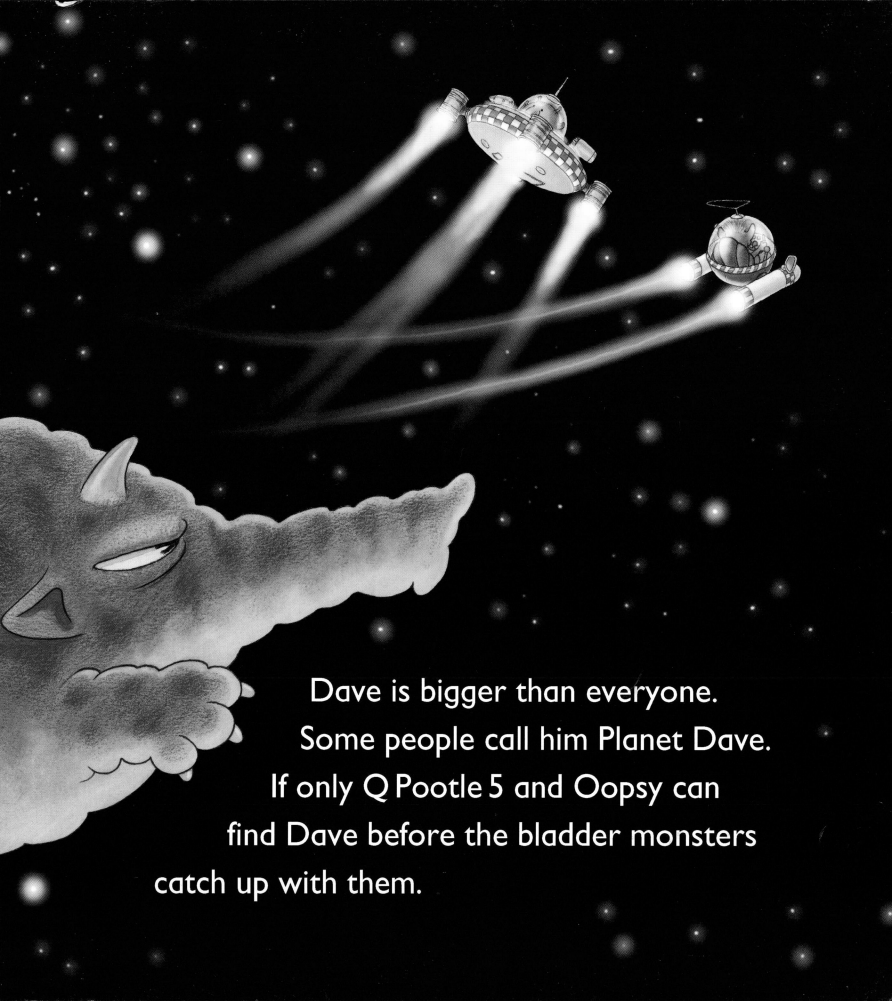

Dave is bigger than everyone.
Some people call him Planet Dave.
If only Q Pootle 5 and Oopsy can
find Dave before the bladder monsters
catch up with them.

Q Pootle 5 and Oopsy land their spaceships.
They wonder which way to go to find Dave.
Suddenly a big, rumbling voice says,
"Hello, Q Pootle 5!
Hello, Oopsy!
How nice of you
to visit."

What luck! Q Pootle 5 and Oopsy have accidentally landed on Dave.

They tell Dave about the bladder monsters
and they hide behind Dave's nose.
The bladder monsters can't see them.
They fly off to search somewhere else.

Dave is very pleased to see his visitors. "I simply don't have enough company," he tells them. He wishes he could be like the really big planets.

"It must be so nice to have moons. To have someone to talk to and to dance with."

"Yes," says Q Pootle 5.

"It must."

Q Pootle 5 feels he should be going. He tells Dave he has never been good at dancing. But he'll come back soon. Oopsy says that she *is* quite good at dancing, but she has to go too.

Q Pootle 5 and Oopsy take off and zoom away. From here, Dave looks quite small. He is almost lost amongst the millions and billions and trillions of stars.

Q Pootle 5 and Oopsy decide to stop
for lunch. They land on an asteroid.
It's nice and peaceful
without those...

BLADDER MONSTERS! Oh dear. And they look really scary. And Dave is a long way away. "B-b-beeebother-b-boootle!" says Q Pootle 5. But Oopsy has a plan.

"You bladder monsters don't scare me,"
she says and she nudges Q Pootle 5.
"No," says Q Pootle 5, "you don't scare her."

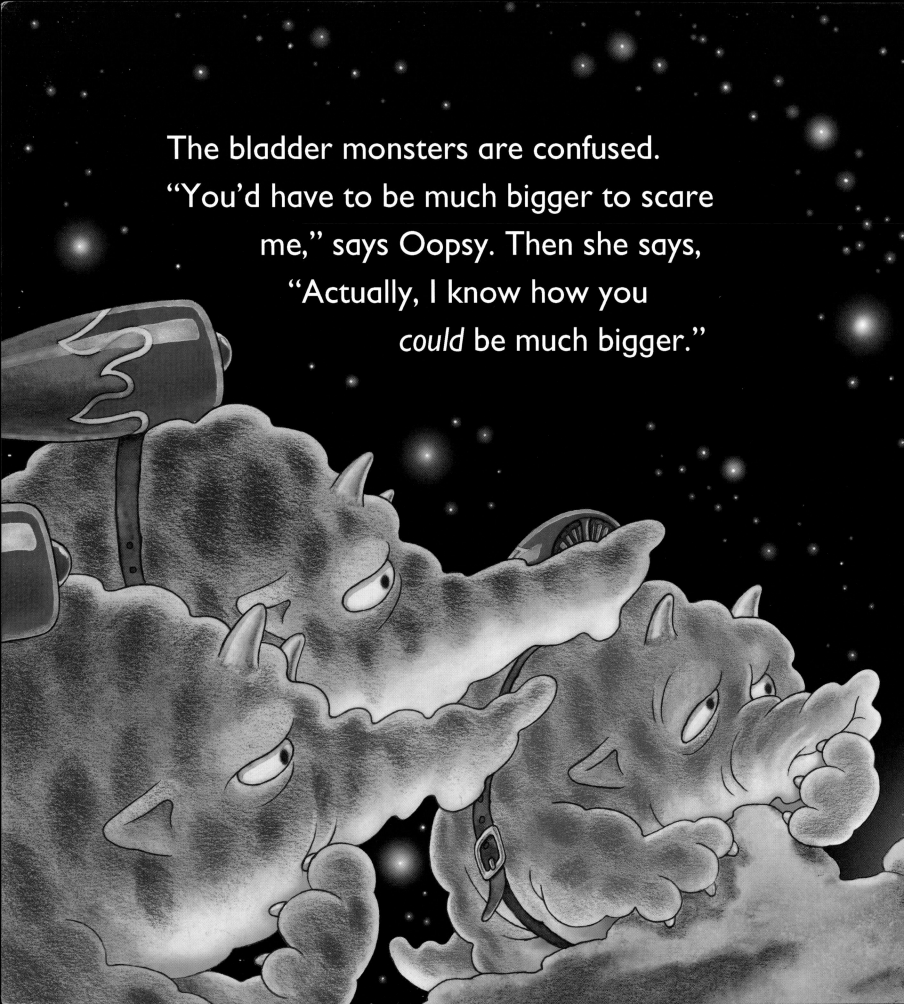

The bladder monsters are confused. "You'd have to be much bigger to scare me," says Oopsy. Then she says, "Actually, I know how you *could* be much bigger."

The bladder monsters are excited.
"Tell us! Tell us!" they say. "Please tell us!"
"Oh, all right," says Oopsy. Q Pootle 5
wonders if this really is a
good idea.

Oopsy whispers to the bladder monsters.
Then she uses one of Q Pootle 5's lateral
stabilising jets to pump up the monsters
to an ENORMOUS size.
"You'll have to hold your breath!"
                                    she tells them.

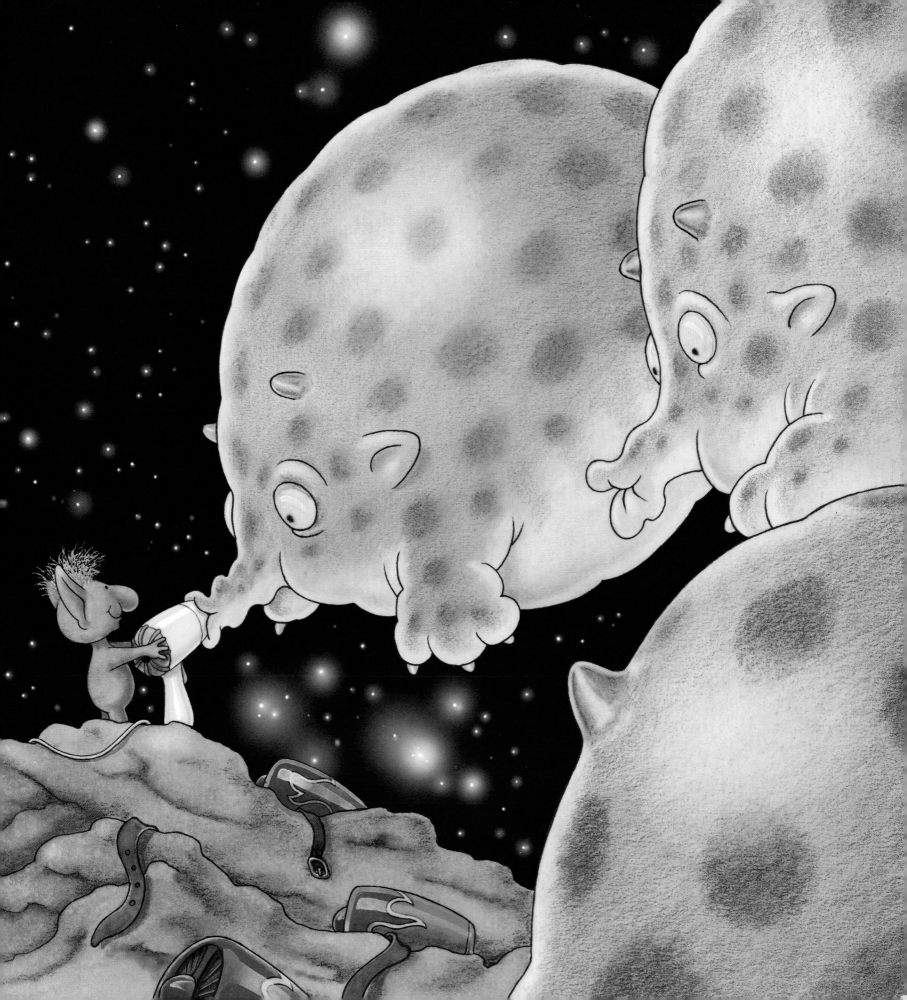

One of the bladder monsters can't. He
suddenly breathes out and flies all over the
place making a rude noise like a balloon . . .

PLPLPLPLPLPWWOOOSSHH!!!

"I'd better tie knots for you,"
says Q Pootle 5, "then you'll stay
pumped up."

Soon the bladder monsters are all pumped up and tied up. Q Pootle 5 has them on strings so they won't blow away.

"What shall we do with them?" Oopsy asks. Q Pootle 5 knows exactly what to do with them . . .

Dave is very pleased
with his bladder monster balloons.
They are not quite as good as
having moons, but they are much
better than having nothing.
Dave wonders if he could teach
them to dance.

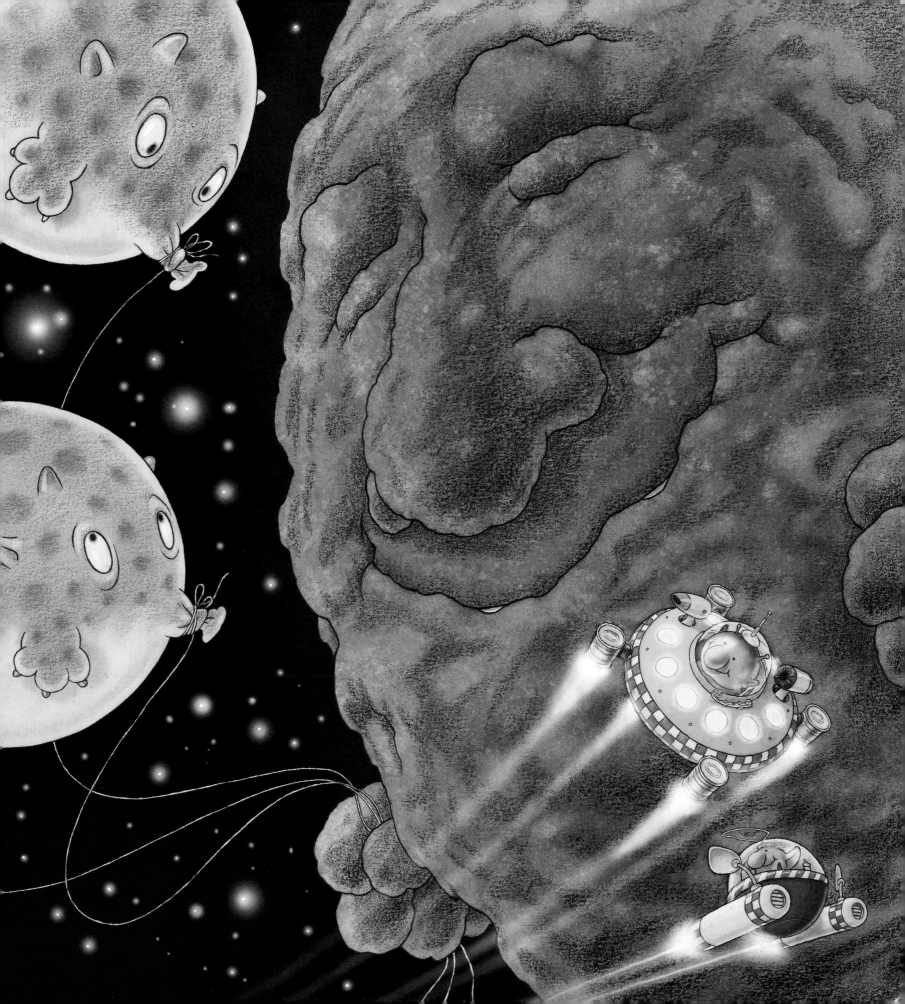

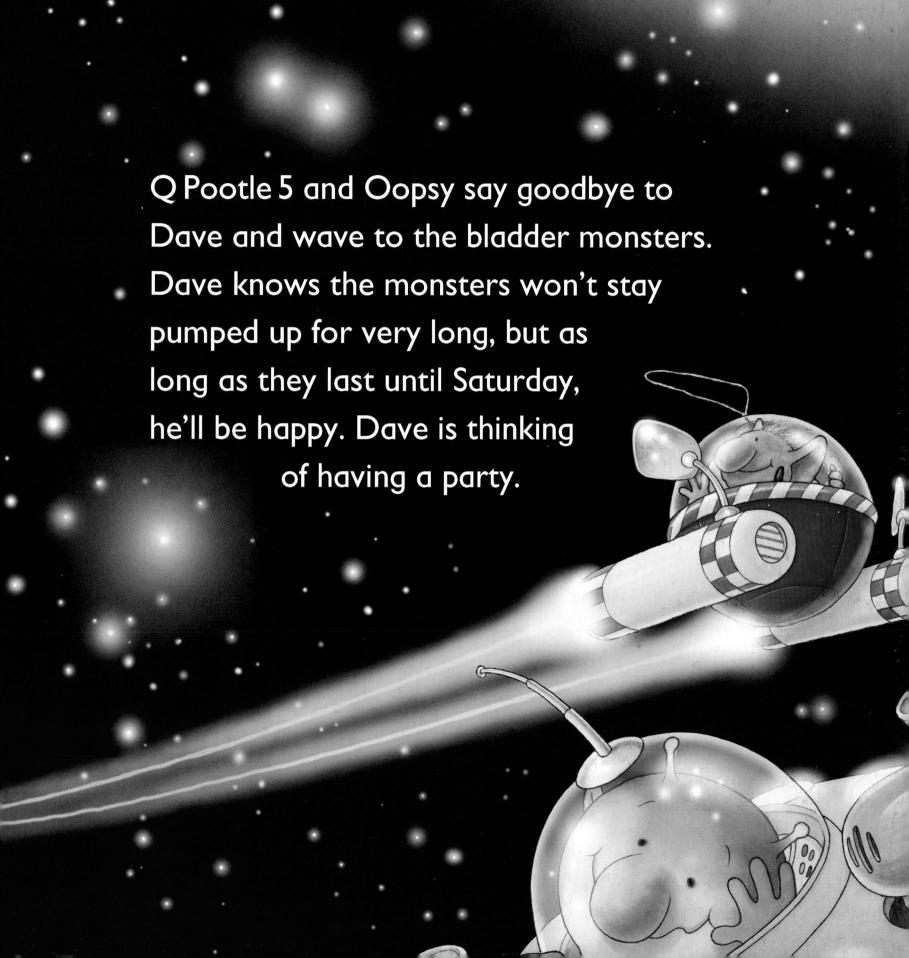

Q Pootle 5 and Oopsy say goodbye to
Dave and wave to the bladder monsters.
Dave knows the monsters won't stay
pumped up for very long, but as
long as they last until Saturday,
he'll be happy. Dave is thinking
of having a party.

As they zoom off into space, Oopsy
radios to Q Pootle 5.
"I could teach you to dance," she says.
"Sorry," says Q Pootle 5. "I can't hear
you very well. I don't think my radio
is working properly. . ."

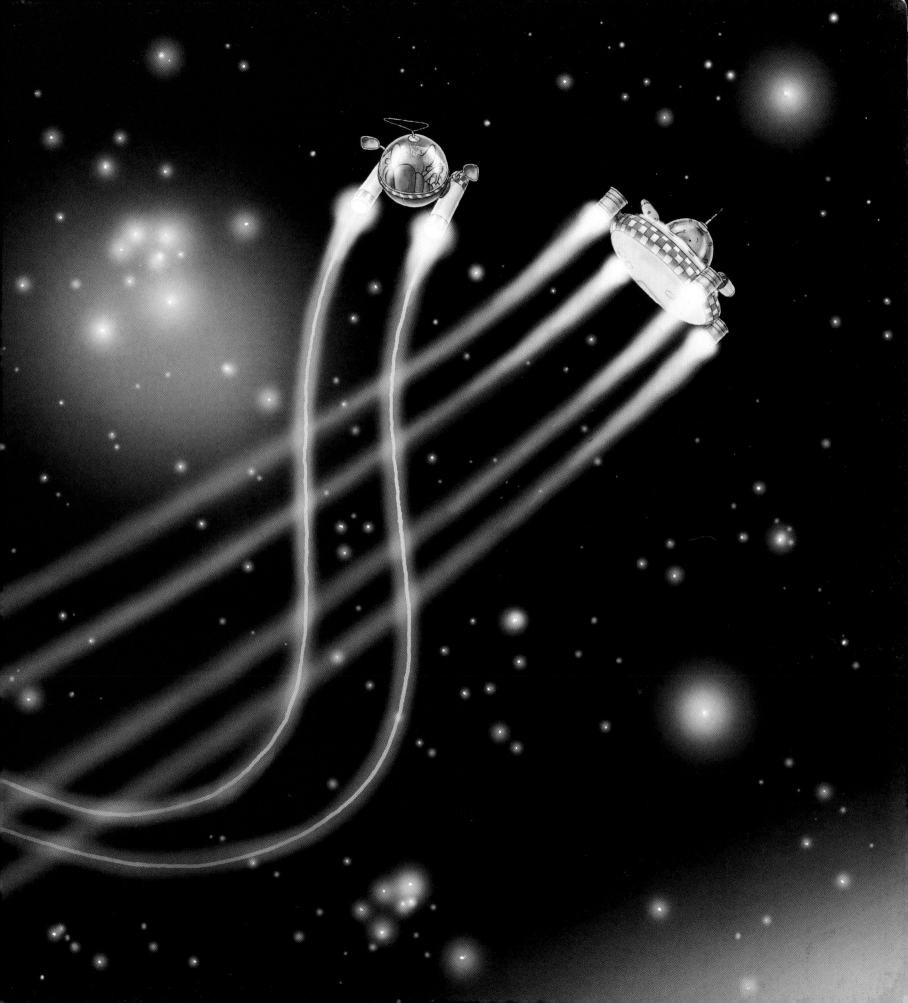

First published in hardback in Great Britain by HarperCollins Publishers Ltd in 2003
First published in paperback by HarperCollins Children's Books in 2004

1 3 5 7 9 10 8 6 4 2

ISBN: 0-00-711973-9

HarperCollins Children's Books is a division of HarperCollins Publishers Ltd.

Text and illustrations copyright © Nick Butterworth 2003

Visit our website at: www.harpercollinschildrensbooks.co.uk

Printed and bound in China